SIXTEEN SHORT STORIES

Sixteen Short Stories

Adolfo Rudy Gelsi

Library of Congress Control Number:		2021918663
ISBN:	Hardcover	978-1-5434-9809-7
	Softcover	978-1-5434-9808-0
	eBook	978-1-5434-9807-3

Rev. date: 09/10/2021

To order additional copies of this book, contact:
Xlibris
844-714-8691
www.Xlibris.com
Orders@Xlibris.com
828058

CONTENTS

A Ghost Story from Littleton, New Hampshire

Littleton, New Hampshire, according to the last survey, is considered one of the most beautiful places to live in America. Located in the White Mountains of New Hampshire with a population of just about six thousand it is the perfect town to retire. Life is very sedentary. The majority of the people know each other. The town is so quiet with no night life to disturb the population. Usually by 7 or 8 o'clock in the evening the town is completely desolated, especially in wintertime. In the summer a few restaurants serve some tourists coming from Canada or any other state close to New Hampshire. I decided to retire to this town after 40 years of working in the city which I do miss some time, but now after five years living in the North Country I am getting used to the life style. This is what happened the night of the 16th of November 2012.

It is seven o'clock on Friday. It snowed all day but now the snow has stopped and it is cold. I check the thermometer outside my window and the mercury has stopped at minus five degrees. I am home alone. My girlfriend went to work at two o'clock and she will work a double shift 16 hours. She will be home 7.30 Saturday morning. Jeopardy has just started on television. It is a show that I have never missed in the last twenty years or so. Usually on Fridays nothing interesting is on television. In the summer months I go outside and work on my property. But in the winter months, because at 5 o'clock it is already dark the only thing to do is watch a good movie or a good show when available. This night, after Jeopardy, I scrolled through all the channels and believe me, nothing interesting was showing. As a writer usually when I have some free time I work on my next book. But this night I was not in the mood for writing or for that matter cooking something for myself, especially on Friday, the day that I don't eat meat because of my religious beliefs. After a few minutes of thinking, I get the local newspaper (Littleton Courier) which I read every week and look through the ads to see if anything is going on in town or any town close by. I know that I don't want to stay home this particular night. I don't care how cold it is or how much snow is on the ground. I have confidence in myself to make it because of my driving record. I never had an accident or any ticket for speeding in my over forty years of driving. Like I said after reviewing all the ads in the paper I find this place located in Franconia, New Hampshire a small town not too far from my house. Driving my usual speed maybe 20 to 30 minute and I would have been there. The name of the place was Cannon Mountain View a Motel Restaurant and Tavern that most of the people use when to make sure that what I was seeing it was really not a mirage. When I got very close to the girl I stop my car completely and I said to myself who is this fool that walks in the middle of the night with the temperature almost zero degrees wearing short sleeves. Usually I don't give rides to anyone unless I know the person, but I felt sorry for that poor girl. I thought to myself maybe she had problem at home, maybe she fought with her husband or boyfriend. I wanted to continue on my way home without getting in any trouble but being a good Christian man I open the window on the passenger side and ask her if she was okay and if she need a ride home in that cold night. I really wanted her to say yes because she was beautiful with long blond hair covering half of her face. I ask her where she was going and she told me that she didn't live far from the cemetery. I asked her where and she told me that she live on North Littleton Road maybe two miles away. I opened the door and told her to get in the car. She got in and I blasted the heat to make her warm. She didn't say a word. I tell you in my life I've been around and saw hundreds of beautiful girls but this one was the most attractive I'd seen in a long time. I was driving very slowly as I didn't want to reach her destination very fast. I asked her name and she told me Marcia and that she lived at 2349 North Littleton Road. She said that she went out with her boyfriend for dinner, they had a fight and the boyfriend told her to walk home and that's what she did. She left the restaurant and started to walk home leaving the coat that she had in the restaurant. I couldn't resist touching her to see if she still was cold. When I touch her she was cold like ice. I stopped my car and took my leather jacket he sees me he gives me a look that I didn't like a bit. I thought what a strange family I have to deal with. I keep my cool and after I said good morning the gentleman that opened the door asked me what I want. I introduced myself and tried to tell why I was there. A few minutes had passed when a lady dressed in black showed up at the front door. Now I had two people to deal with. Very politely I asked if Marcia was up and if she would give me my jacket. At my request both the guy and the lady looked at each other maybe thinking I was crazy. After a pause the gentleman looked at me and asked if I would repeat what I just said. I asked in a very polite way if we can go inside and talk because it was very cold and it would have taken some time to explain everything I had to say. They invited me in and we went into the kitchen. We all sat down and I started to tell them what had happened the night before. I left nothing out and I was very honest about everything. After I finished talking the lady left the kitchen and in few minutes she came back with a picture she presented to me and asked if that picture was the girl that I had given a ride the night before and given her my jacket to keep her warm. When I saw the picture I confirmed that that was her, and that she had my jacket and that I wanted back or I would call the police. At the same time I was talking I can see that the faces of both them changed color, and their eyes turned red and tears started coming down their cheeks. I didn't know what to do. I started to realize that something wrong. I didn't know what had made them so upset that they started to cry. I asked them if I said something that offended them. I would have apologized. They both reassured me that it was nothing I said that made them so upset. The lady left the kitchen table and came back few minutes later with a newspaper clipping. She gave it to me and said to please look at it and read it. I couldn't believe my eyes when I started to read what was on that piece of newspaper. Never in my entire life had I shaken or cried but when I finished reading my body started to shake, tears started to come down and I for a moment lost my speech. I didn't know what to say. I wanted to run out of that house, that article that I had just finished reading was a notice of death of a young girl named Marcia (I will keep the last name private for respect of the family) that had died two years earlier in a car accident. She had lived in Littleton, North Littleton Road # 2584. That corresponded to the truth of everything that Marcia told me the night before. All of us, her mother, father and I stood quiet for few moments. None of us wanted to believe what had just happened. We were petrified at the event. I was ready to leave but before I left the house I asked Marcia's father if he might know where my jacket went. Marcia's father looked at his wife and talked to me saying he couldn't give me an answer he didn't know, but for sure my jacket wasn't in this house. I stood up, turned around and was on my way out of that house. I was close to the front door, I turned toward Marcia's father if we could take a ride to the Wheeler Hill Cemetery where Marcia's grave is. He said he would and he told his wife that we would be back in ten minutes. He drove down because I had no car. When we got into the gate of the cemetery he parked the car and we walked right where Marcia grave was. We couldn't believe our eyes when we got close. There were no words to describe what

Women Take Over

I was very suspicious, I could feel it in my blood that something was going to happen. For the last couple of weeks after dinner, my three women (my wife and two daughters) would all sit down and talk behind my back when I would leave the kitchen. At first I paid no attention. I thought it was the usual conversation of women, just chat about anything that happened during the day. But after some time went by, I noticed that every time I approached the kitchen, all of them would laugh and stop talking. For a while I let it go, but with time it started to get unbearable and I decided to confront all three.

One night after dinner I went into the living room, then as they started to chat I went back into the kitchen. As soon as they saw me they stopped talking. I said, "Please don't stop now. If I'm not mistaken, I live in this house, too, and I believe that I should know what's going on in my house. It's me who pays the bills, goes to work every day, and makes sure everything is okay. I hope you all understand that I would like to know why you all start to chat every time I leave the kitchen. I do believe you all respect me with your hearts and I also believe that you all don't talk about me behind my back. But I would like an explanation of why you all stop talking when you see me."

I didn't even get to finish my sentence when I was interrupted by my daughter Rachel, the most outspoken, She is very open when she talks about what the young generation says. "Dad!! We were waiting for this day for a long time. We knew sooner or later you were going to confront us. We are very happy that you confronted us. For starters, we want to tell you that we love you very much. You are the person that we love more than anything else in this world. We would give our lives for you, and that should assure you about our chat every night after dinner. My dear Papa, I can tell you right now that you will be against everything we talk about. Mama, please tell Dad that he's got nothing to do with our conversation and that we are not trying to change the rules in this house.

My wife looks at me in a different way than she usually does. Then with a deep, almost baritone, voice she expressed her way.

"My dear husband, I am sure that what I'm going to tell you you're not going to like, but please pay attention and hear me out. We women of today's world are tired of being treated like second rate. In everything that happens in today's social life, we try to organize ourselves like a lot of organizations out there are trying to do. We as women would like to take part in one of these organizations. This is what we talk about when we get together. The men in today's world want to control everything; they make their own rules. If the women try to contradict any of these rules, we get in trouble. It has been a long time that we've kept our mouths shut and just listened. We absorb lots of lies coming through from every corner of the country. My dear husband, look around, you read the paper. Look at everything that happens daily. I'm sure that you see the power that men have. It will not take us to a better future. I hope that this big conference next month in Japan on human rights will give us women a chance to get up on a platform and express ourselves, make the world listen to us and let us be a part of this society. We want to have a place in government and to try to correct everything that men have demolished in the last seventy years.

"Since the end of the second war you men sink everything in regards to politics. You men use nuclear energy and create lots of garbage that pollutes the air we breathe daily. We women always were left sitting on the side with our ideals sacrificed, without any the possibility of expressing ourselves. I think that your daughters and I have the right to speak about everything. Women should take over and all the men should be in the kitchen. We need to straighten out this world. We need a change. We need somebody that understands today's people. People suffer so deeply in this society, it's time to change; no more wars, this way is out of date. We women do not accept war. For us the nuclear age needs to be abolished. We make love rather than accept war. We can straighten out the monetary balance and deficit and we are capable of governing this country. If man were to transfer governing power to the women we would change the world. Remember, as women we have always made the rules and governed in the family household. We make sure that our kids are raised with ideals and respect. We always control the money that our husbands bring home weekly. We check and balance the interest of our revenue. Our family survives.

"Give us the chance to rule over the nation's capital, and you will see the results of change we'll bring to mankind. We will live in peace. The people will then smile as they wake to the new rays of the morning sun. I'm almost positive this will come to pass if we take over. This is what me and your daughters discuss every day after dinner and we really think your presence is unnecessary. We don't want to create a hitch in our family just because we interpret things in a different way than you do. I'm sure that in time the world will progress and war will be erased from the dictionary."

I listen to my wife without interruption. I do not agree with everything she says, but to tell the truth she did make some sense. It is time that we men start to have some respect. We cannot use women as we please and then throw them away like a used object. I hope that the conference in Japan goes on their favor. I know that the majority of the men will not accept that and eventually will say that now that all the women in the world are equal to men they will destroy us, and let us be paid for everything that we did to them in the last two hundred years.

I relaxed for a minute and then with a lot of respect I asked my wife to prepare some coffee. She noticed the different approach that I used when I asked her and without hesitation she started to make the coffee. When the coffee was ready she called me. I fixed the coffee the way I like it and went into the living room. I sat on the sofa and started to think. "Why would I get upset if the world changed? We need a change! For me it shouldn't make a difference. I should be happy because I have three women in my house and maybe things can be better. I see who rules my home is my wife. Every week I give her my check, my daughters go out any time they please; it is hard to control them, they dress the way they want.

I don't think the situation can get any worse than it is right now. I speak out loud to all the men. "Let's give them the responsibility, lets give them the problems of the world, let them take over the world, let them say whatever they want. Let them call us men when they need us, let them say when they want to make love and have a baby, let them find the ideal way to approach life, let them put on the pants and we put on the dress. It should make no difference, we know that in the universe the majority of the population are women. To be exact, for every man there are seven women. Just on numbers alone, we men are the minority. Let's live in peace, relax and go to work. Let's make ourselves something to eat, let's make ourselves coffee the way we want it, let the women take over. Let them meet the needs of the new generation in this corrupt world."

I start to get tired and fall asleep. I reach over to my wife and kid, and I say I agree with you all! I hope the rest of the world listens too!

Me and My Vegetable Garden

My name is Giovanni, but everybody calls me John. I used to work, but a few years back I had an accident on my job -- a serious accident that has left me unable to work. Now that I feel a little better I want to try and make myself useful around the house and get some personal satisfaction. This year I firmly decided what I wanted to do in the spring time. For the last few years I have been thinking of making a vegetable garden in back of my house.

The first thing that I did before I started my new project was to watch my neighbor who is retired and very competent about growing vegetables.. Once in awhile I ask him a few questions about gardening. I see him every spring preparing his soil before putting seeds in. He is good. He told me that for the last ten years he has never gone to the supermarket to buy vegetables and he has saved a lot of money. Now that I feel little better I would like to try and maybe I can save some money. In my house it is just me and my wife but believe me at the end of the month if we do not make sacrifices sometimes we cannot pay our bills.

I did not even tell my wife what my intentions were. I am a man who doesn't ask anyone when I've decided to do something. That's what I did.

One morning as soon as I got up from bed, after I drank my espresso coffee, I went to wake my wife. I went into the back of the house where my wife had a beautiful garden full of flowers. Without making a lot of noise I started to pull all the flowers to make room for my vegetable garden. To be honest I felt very sad, but then I said to myself if I want to save some money it is better that I plant some vegetables because you can't eat flowers. Especially in the winter when we go to buy beans, carrots, broccoli, and other vegetables, it costs us an arm and a leg.

Anyway, as I said, I was pulling the flowers when my wife appeared at the window that looks down on the garden. As soon she saw what I was doing, she started to scream so loudly that all the neighbors came out of their houses. Everyone thought that someone had died, or that the end of the world was near. I tried to calm her down, but unsuccessfully. I decided to go inside the house to explain to her that what I was doing was good for us, that eventually we would save some money with all the vegetables that we would pick. Finally she agreed with me and I went back into the garden to finish cleaning. It was a hard job because the roots were so deep and I knew that the soil was supposed to cleansed of impurities to produce good vegetables. It took me a few days, but in the end I was very happy with the job that I had done. I did it exactly the way my neighbor told me.

The day came that my garden was ready to be planted, I went to the store to buy whatever was necessary. When I got there I told the owner what my intentions were, that I needed some tools to start a new vegetable garden. The owner replied, "Not to worry! I got everything that you need. If you have a little patience I will take care of you." I was in the store for about one hour looking around. I never saw so many tools in my life, he had everything you could imagine, but finally he called me next to the counter and started to show me everything that I need for my garden. When I saw all the tools, all the bags, all the sprays I was already discouraged to start this new project. But then I said to myself this is money that I will spend just one time and over the years that I will use them again; it money well spent. I paid for all that stuff. A young kid helped me put everything in the car.

On my way home I was thinking how to tell my wife about all that money that I spent, but I was in luck because when I got home the wife wasn't there. I started to work immediately and was thinking that if my wife would come home she would see me working and couldn't complain that I never do anything. I started to scatter the fertilizer; I doused it with water to make sure the garden was well wet, and I waited for sunset before I started to plant my vegetables. That's what my neighbor told me that you should never plant before sunset; that was the old-fashioned way. A few hours later my wife came home and the first thing she did was to come in the back of the house and see all the work that I did. She just said, "Good job and good luck with the garden." The sunset came and I started to plant my vegetables, I started with the tomatoes, then I put some salad, some beans, some celery and some other vegetables. When I was finished I went inside the house to wash up and get a bite to eat. As soon as she saw me the wife started to tell me that with all the tomatoes that I planted she would put them in the bottles and save them for the winter. She would do the same with the peppers, beans and other vegetables.

I was very proud of what I had done and every morning I would go to the garden to water it and pull the weeds. It was a new way for me to spend some time without nothing. The days were going fast. The plants were growing very beautifully, even my neighbor was jealous of the way my plants were growing. He said. "You will see that all the work that you did will give you some satisfaction and lots of vegetables."

I believed everything that he said because nobody knew better than he. The time passed and I thought at last I will make my wife happy every day when she tells me to go into the garden and pick some vegetables to make a salad or to use some tomatoes for the gravy. Every morning I went into the garden to see if any fruit of my hard work would finally appear; but it was the same very morning. My plants were beautiful, all full of leaves, I would tell my wife to have patience. Eventually we would have a lot of vegetables.

The days went by, the summer ended, my beautiful plants started to dry up, it was almost time to pull them out of the ground and the only vegetables that I picked were two tomatoes and a few carrots. It was really bad. My wife was mad; she screamed every day that I was going into the garden; she had all the right in the world to get mad. I destroyed that flower garden that she worked for years to make the way it was. I also spent a lot of money on tools and seed, and I can tell you that for that money that I spent I would have bought at least one ton of tomatoes and other vegetables. I was keeping my mouth shut every time she said something. I felt bad enough that all my work was for nothing, that all the seeds that I planted died without giving me any fruit.

But reflecting a little, I knew that in life one can expect anything. Because what happened to me in my garden is just the same as what happens in a family evolution. We are born, we grow, we plant the seed for a new life, but -- let's be honest -- who can guarantee that the seed that we plant will give us the fruit that we expect?

VACATION

It is July. Usually, this is the time my family and I go on vacation. After working so hard all year long, we take the month of July and go out of the city to relax.

But this year before I made the final decision about the family vacation, I had some serious thought about staying home. I knew that would not be an easy dilemma to resolve. I was thinking and thinking, hoping to come up with a definite answer, wondering how to approach my family who were so adjusted to the yearly ritual. I started by talking to myself in the hope that I might come up with a solution.

"Is this vacation really necessary?" I asked myself. I am not a young man any more. I do not agree with the younger generation's definition of the word "vacation." They think it means not coming home at night, drinking, going to night clubs, speed racing. When I was young, vacation meant a time to be united with one's family all day and think about the year ahead, and mostly relax. Today's vacations are . . . . . What are today's vacations? Honestly I do not know because millions of families every year have the same problem. They ask themselves,

"Is this vacation really necessary? Many vacations are just a way of squandering money that might be used for better things; for example, we might need it later to help the kids when they are adults. Unfortunately, in these modern times I can't talk like that with my kids, for they would not understand. They see the vacation in a different way. They are young, and we are from different generations.

When we were young we used ethical principles to guide us when we went on vacation. The word "vacation" for us had just one meaning -- to relax absolutely after a year of intense work, either physical or mental.

Relaxation? Nothing could be farther from the reality. When my family and I get to a vacation spot, relaxing is just a dream. In the past years on our vacation everything except relaxation happened. . My kids are very selfish and do not care about anything. I am the one who does all the work -- every day, same routine. I go to the supermarket and shop for food, go to the beach and see that we get a spot where we get some sun. This really makes me mad, but I can do nothing about it. My wife does not want to know about my problems.

You can understand then why this year I would like to stay home. But before I make any final decision, I must discuss the situation with my family. I already have an idea how this discussion will go. I imagine that before I can open my mouth, my kids will have something to say, something that would make it seem as though they are paying for the vacation or perhaps might be making some physical contribution.

First I tell my wife that we should have a family

conversation -- just me, her, and the two kids -- to discuss my intention. She agrees and the following night all four of us sat in the living room. Before I could even open my mouth my oldest daughter interrupts me. "I know why you gathered us here. It is because you want to talk about the vacation we go on every year."

This made me very angry, and without hesitation I raised my tone of voice and said, "You are right. This meeting is about the vacation. I am tired of going on vacation every year and not enjoying so much as one day. I know why you want to go on vacation: just because you are seventeen you think you can do everything you like. In the past years I have never seen you help anyone. You just go to the beach where your friends wait for you, put on your swimsuit that is so scanty it makes passersby turn their heads and gives them the strangest ideas. But I, your father, can say nothing about it because as soon as I start to talk, you interrupt me and start to use words that didn't even exist when I was an adolescent."

At that moment my son just looked at me. He did not even try to open his mouth because I preceded him by saying, "You (pointing at him) are fifteen years old and already think you are an adult. Every day you ask for money. You would think that money is falling from the sky. You say that there is something you need every day because all your friends have money in their pockets, and you can't go out with them if you don't have money in your pockets. If by any chance you should meet a girl you can't even buy an ice cream."

My wife usually never says anything. She just listens; but I already know that in the end she will express herself. She just waits for me to finish talking, and then asks the kids if they have anything to say before she starts talking. I finally told my family my intention about staying home for this year's vacation. My wife looked at me and started to talk, first with my daughter who has taken offense at my harsh words. .

My dear daughter started, "You should know about going on vacation. Do you remember what happened last year when we went to the beach? the salt water? The sun is not healthy for your delicate skin. You should remember the consequences that you went through; and you should remember that program we saw on TV where a scientist was talking about the environmental atmosphere. They were talking about the hole in the ozone, the dangers of staying in the sun, the consequences of getting skin cancer, and of other illnesses which could occur in the future."

My wife picked up. "My dear, I do understand that after a year in school, that after a year of this noisy city, after a year of problems, doctor bills, and many more things, we need a vacation. But to be honest I think I have a solution for all the family. I think a cruise would be the best thing. We could stay all together, enjoy the sunsets, talk as a family by the light of the moon. This is something we have never done at home. This for me is the only solution for this year. I hope your father likes the idea."

I was listening to everything my wife was suggesting. I was sipping a glass of good homemade wine; but in my thoughts I was trying to figure out how much money all this would cost. My mind was confused, but suddenly everything stopped. Suppose the vacation were to be abolished altogether!

What an idea! I could relax, pay all my debts. I could buy a new suit (it is over ten years since I last bought a suit). For a month I could feel like a millionaire. I could wake up at midday. After dinner, I could go to the cafe and sip a nice Italian espresso or cappuccino with my friends I have not seen in ages. I could take a long walk in the afternoon when the sun is setting. At night I could read a book before I go to bed, I could make love to my wife the way I used to, not rushing because in the morning I have to get up early to go to work.

This is just a dream, a daytime dream, that will never be a reality. I know that nobody in my family will accept my suggestion of how I want to spend my vacation. I know that when it is vacation time, I, as husband and father, have to sacrifice myself and follow the wishes of my family, The vacation negates any right I have to be the boss in my house.

I know that this is not a win-win situation. I have to give in and make my family happy, and pay the financial consequences after the fact.

Just like that, after my last sip of homemade wine, I turned toward my wife and children, and I said, "Please, all of you make up your mind where we are going on vacation. Just let me know how much this vacation will cost, and if I am short with the money tomorrow, I will go to the bank and ask for a loan. But remember one thing. After the vacation is over, all of us have to pitch in to pay this loan back to the bank."

Then I went on to say, "Here is one simple solution. Every

Matrimonial Crisis

It was a cool day in the middle of the week. As usual Mark got in his car to go at the cafe and have his espresso coffee. As soon he got there he saw Mario sitting at one of the tables reading the newspaper. He had met Mario a few months earlier at the house of a mutual friend. Mark was very courteous; before he ordered his coffee, he went over to Mario to say hello to him.

Mark: Hi Mario! Do you remember me? How are you doing?

Mario: Of course I remember you! We met at Robert's house. How do you do? Sit down, let me buy you a coffee. Bartender, please see what my friend wants.

Mark: Thank you, let me have an espresso. Thank you.

Mario: Well, tell me, have you seen Robert lately?

Mark: Yes, I saw Robert, and I must tell you that he has been acting very strange lately. It is not his health, but something is worrying him. The last time I saw him he told me a story that shocked me. If you give me a few minutes I would like to tell you what happened. Maybe we can help him to find a solution.

Mario: (interrupting Mark) You can count on me if I can help. Just tell me what's going on with Robert.

Mark: I am sorry, Mario. Let me get to the point. I believe you know Robert well, right?

Mario: Yes! I have known Robert for a long time. We went to school together. Why do you ask me such question? I hope nothing has happened to him.

Mark: No nothing happened to him physically, but let me tell you what happened last time I saw him.

Mario: Let me hear what you got to say, and maybe I can give you an answer, and maybe try to help our friend.

Mark: Robert is a good man, he is a hard-working man. His family is a priority in his life, he never argues with anyone, he is a man of integrity, he adores his wife, and his kids. He can't stop talking about his kids, he is so proud of them sometimes I am jealous. He's got the perfect family. You can see that in his tone of voice and the look he has on his face. Well, let me tell you what happened last week. As usual I came to the cafe to get my espresso coffee. There I saw Robert. As soon he saw me, he invited to sit at his table and offered to buy my coffee. I could tell that something was wrong by the way he looked. He told me that he wanted to talk if I had some time. As a good friend I agreed to sit at his table to listen to what he had to tell me. Without hesitation he started to talk about his family. He told me that he has been trying for the last few weeks to talk with his wife, but he can't find the right words to start the conversation. He's really worried about what he read in the local newspaper that he buys every day. I told him to not worry, because most of the time authors write fantasy to make people buy the newspaper. I tell you, my dear friend Mario, when I told Robert not to believe every thing he read, he got offended. Because I consider myself one of his best friends, I listened to what he had to tell me, to what it was that was bothering him so much. I was sipping my coffee when he started to tell me what he read in the newspaper. He started by saying, "Please let me explain to you what really bothers me. I hope you will listen, you know that I have a lot of respect for our friendship. If you can help me resolve this problem that I have since I read the article, I would really appreciate it. Listen please. You know that everyday I buy the newspaper, I have been doing that as far back as I can remember because I really believe that by reading you would learn how to express yourself. Also it is a way to keep in contact with the outside world. By reading the paper you will have a sense of communication, have a better sense of culture, learn new concepts in life that change everyday. If you don't believe me, listen what I read the other day: This article was very specific saying that in a period of our life existence will approach an **indigent** stage. This is not just for humans, but true for the animals as well. By **indigent** stage I mean separation. According to this article, this indigent stage is so prehistoric in its origins that it cannot be changed even if we live in the twentieth century. It is in everyone's genes. I read that in any case of cohabitation in a relationship after a certain period we come to outgrow each other. One aspect of this disturbing phenomenon is that it can happen in a marriage." Robert continued to say that since he read this article, his brain was so confused, that the idea was there in his vision night and day. He was going insane because he could not accept that particular theory that eventually he would distance himself from his family. He read that at first you start to notice the waning of closeness shown by the companion, (in this case, his wife). He read that she would feel very annoyed every time he would try to get close to her. "I really believe, my dear friend, that I cannot live like that for a long period of time.," he said. "I must resolve this situation in the best way I can. I know that after a few days I would start to feel my seclusion from my family. I know that a situation like that can bring more turbulent words. One of them is divorce. I cannot cope with such a situation. I have been married for over ten years, and I do not want to ever mention the word divorce. Under the circumstance I would prefer to die before I would divorce my wife. I also want to tell you that if this would happen I would prefer to send my wife to her parents for a period of time and have a friendly separation, send her away with the kids. I am sure that the time would fly away very fast, and after we would come back together and start over again like newlyweds on the first night of the honeymoon. I think that any new way to approach life would be different and our love would fly to new horizons." This is the essence of what he said. My dear friend do you understand what I just finished telling you? I have tried to simplify all that talk that Robert did, but without success. I listened to him for over one hour. Tell me, what do you think about all this?

Mario: To be honest I do not know what to say. I would like to help him but usually I don't get involved in family matters. I will keep my eyes open just in case.

Mark: I think you are right I will do the same. I will follow the case, but I will not get involved I don't want to give Robert any of my ideas. In fact he told me that he would talk to his wife. Let's just follow this matter from the outside. Let's just see what happens. (Mark looks at his watch.) Holy . . .! Time flew away very fast. I've got to go; it was nice to see you again, I will keep in touch, let's see what happens to Robert. Good bye for now!

A few days later at Robert's house. Robert has come home from work. As usual he kisses his wife Gina and kids, washes up before he takes his favorite spot in the kitchen, waiting for his wife to serve him his meal the same way that she has been doing since they got married. After dinner Robert ask the kids to leave the kitchen because he had something to discuss with his wife. The kids respectively left the kitchen, Robert told his wife to leave the table the way it was and to sit next to him because he had something to talk about. Gina sits next to her husband. Robert, looks at his wife very intensely, then he caresses her face and starts to tell her every thing that he told his friend Mark. His wife at first listens without any interruption. She was too stunned at her husband's words to utter a word. After a few minutes she regained her composure and came to reality and spoke:

Gina: Robert!!! Please!!! stop!!! I do not know what you are talking about, I do not understand any of the words that you say, maybe it's a different language that I am hearing. Is this you talking? The same Robert that I met fifteen years ago, and the one I married ten years ago? Please stop! Are you okay? Would you like me to make an appointment for you with the doctor? Maybe you are starting to lose your mind.

(Robert was frozen from his wife's words. He didn't try to stop her, he just listened, he knew that he made a mistake to tell his wife about his marriage possibly breaking up. Gina continued talking but her voice started to soften, especially after she looked at her husband and saw his face change completely. After a few minutes of talking she started to laugh, it was a beautiful laugh that was coming out of her smiling face. At the same time she got very close to Robert and continued to say:]

Gina: My dear husband, just stay calm; don't get agitated. I don't want to lose you from a heart attack. I don't believe a word of the story that you read in the newspaper. I believe in the sacrament of Holy Matrimony. Yes, I know that time has changed us, but I am still thinking the antic ways. Believe me I am never going to change my ways of thinking. I still remember when my mother was telling me: "My dear daughter, when you get married, you will make your own new bed and whatever the circumstances you have to sleep in that bed." Now I tell you it is too late for repentance. I made my bed with you and I've got to sleep on it. Marriage is not a honeymoon that is over after a few days. The marriage is a holy sacrament that is broken only with death. You've got to understand that. Not every day of our lives we will laugh. We will try to make every day the best of our life. I am sure that we will have some really dark days; but we've got to go on. We are a good family. You are a good husband, I think I am a good wife and a good mother, we've got two beautiful kids that we adore. We've got a house; we live comfortably. You've got to have a little patience, we must make ourselves available to understand each other. I do not believe in this crisis that you are talking about. We love each other, we are made to be happy, to educate our kids the best way we can. I'll tell you one more time, please forget this article you read. Just think that never happened. And now that the kids are outside playing, please come with me into the bedroom and I will show you that we have no crisis, and that the phrase "matrimonial crisis" between us is nonexistent.

THE ACCUSATION

Everybody knows that the words of our mothers are always right. Mothers make sense, they have instinct, they try in any way to make us understand the changes and degradation that have been occurring in this world in the last twenty years. I see it, I feel it inside me, it's perceived in the morning air when I wake up.

When I was young this discussion didn't make any sense. Today we need a guide to wake us up from this nightmare that we live in every day. I think that the best words to a resolution are the words that came from our mothers' mouths. These words keep us aware of the adventure that we live every day and keep us alert to the weaknesses of certain individuals.

I remember my mother repeating the same words hundreds of times. In record time she would say, "Watch out! Do not make any mistakes. Now that you are on your own, remember my words. You have a good job, think about your future. Sacrifice yourself for what you have and try to get some personal satisfaction."

My father, a man of few words with old-fashioned principles, once in a while would preach to me in a superficial way. He would say, "Please have personality. Do not take anything for granted. Even if it looks easy and innocent, be patient. Keep a cool temper before you take steps that you would regret for the rest of your life and that could destroy your future."

I remember we used to sit at the kitchen and after my mother finished cleaning up, she would make a nice cup of coffee and my father would start to talk in a soft voice. "I know that a man is always a man, but sometimes he has to control himself. The consequences can inevitably cause him risks in the future. We as parents want the best; we want to be proud. We want to give a good example to all who are weak or have a libertine mentality."

I would listen to every word my father spoke. I had very little experience with the outside world. I was frightened to hear my father speak; but he was right, every word made sense.

From time to time I would talk to my grandfather, a man with idealistic views, but with a good sense of humor. I knew that when he was young he was well respected in every way. He would never back off for any reason. He would say what he wanted to, and he intended people to hear him, not to misunderstand anything he said. Some people told me about the love affair of my grandfather. He had no rivals, he was so simple that people accepted him for his good example.

I remember we would sit on the step by the back door, the one close to the garden and admire its beauty. It had the most elegant adornments of flowers. My grandfather spent part of his day caring for the garden. It showed the architectural touch of a man with lots of experience.

I remember sitting there one afternoon when it was so calm and tranquil. The rays of the sun beat down on the field, a soft wind was moving the reeds not far from where my grandfather and I sat. It was paradise! That was the first time that I confided in my grandfather. That afternoon I would ask him for an explanation to help me understand why my father would say and repeat every time he spoke to me. "Please be careful." I didn't understand what this meant! My mother, using a different approach, would say every morning repeatedly "Please do not make a mistake." I told my grandfather, "I do try to control everything I do, I am very scrupulous in my actions, particularly when I'm outside my father's warmth."

My grandfather listened without interruption. I expected him to interrupt any minute; but instead he listened and I continued to talk and express myself:

"I do not understand! I'm twenty years old. I feel the heat and the agitation. I feel the desire. I'm sure, dear Grandfather, that when you were my age you felt the same way. I must tell you that where I work and spend a lot of my time, I see a lot of strange things. It isn't like my mother and father think it is. I do not see all the respect that they talk about every day. The language is not as polite as it was twenty years ago; it is more open now. Even the women do not have modesty or reserve in their language like my mother and father do. Sometimes the girls give me lots of compliments on my looks. I do accept them with exuberance even if I do not express myself with libertine ways. I do understand from the tone of their voices that they are trying to proposition me. They say, 'Come on, don't you see that I like you? Please do not tell me that you do not like women!'

"Sometimes I think I should change my ways of thinking. Listen, Grandfather, my boss is a lady -- beautiful and very elegant. She is a widow. She has a sophisticated language. You can tell by the way she dictates orders in the office that she has no problem expressing herself in a tough way. The other day my boss asked me to stay late. She told me that some paperwork was not done properly and it had to be done that day. To be honest, I didn't want to stay but she was very persuasive in making me stay. Her beautiful eyes told me not to refuse. Erotic ideas passed through my mind. Sometimes these ideas make me feel like a real man with a desire that a man can't suppress.

"When she invited me to stay late at the office, I started to feel exuberant. I began to plot how I might seduce this beautiful woman. This would certainly give me a lot of motivation to go to work at the office every day. I was confused. I knew that if I stayed in the office with her, something more than paperwork would happen. In that moment I didn't know what to do. My body was telling me to stay with her, and the frantic passion of my masculinity was telling me to break all the rules. My mother and father's words came into my mind. I didn't want to disappoint them. I love them very much, and they are everything to me in my life. Not to disappoint them is one of my principles in life.

"At that moment of mental confusion I thanked my lady boss for the offer and told her that it was impossible for me to stay because that night I had other commitments. She couldn't have imagined the way my body reacted to the renunciation of the offer. Maybe she felt the same way; I couldn't tell! That day she smiled at me and with a gentle voice thanked me and said, 'Maybe some other time.'

"When she left the office, my body transformed into the master, and my mental resolve weakened. A physical obsession was pursuing me. I repeated to myself a hundred times, 'Are you a man or what? Suppose she never asks you to stay again. I really think that I lost a good opportunity. How stupid I am.'

"Tell me, grandfather, what do you think? What would you have done? Should I have accepted her invitation?"

My grandfather continued to listen without interruption. He took his time to respond, and it seemed to me he was in meditation. The he lit a cigar, savored the smell of the tobacco and looked at me and said with a soft voice; "My dear grandchild, remember that the wolf loses his fur not his vice. I can tell you that when I was young it was the same. Lots of times I was asked to be with women, but it was in a different manner. Those were different times -- although time does not change the way women try to catch men. They have a special way of approaching the situation. They have a quality that we men don't have.

"Furthermore," my grandfather continued, "I'd like to be specific on one thing. In my time when something like that happened nobody cared. Yes, you would hear some murmuring, but nothing more. We didn't have all these laws that make you kids crazy. Today when you start a relationship with someone you have to watch every move you make, every word that you say. I do not disagree with the laws, but I can give you some facts on how to be a man. I personally think that you should never refuse the invitation of a woman -- most importantly, if it's your boss. As a man you've got to do what you've got to do. Live the passion of the moment. You know that what your boss was asking for was just your body, not a relationship. If you were good, maybe you would make love a few more times, and then when she got tired of you, she would trash you like a piece of meat. You, on the other hand, have to play the game. She is a woman; she can do anything; she can see you at work every day. If you tried to act indifferent, she could get rid of you. She could say that you sexually molested her. You know that would be out of guilt and spite because no one would believe that she was the one that started this amazing story. I suggest that if you'd like to save your reputation as a man you should leave your job and find another place to work. When life starts to get complicated, there is no other solution."

I listened to my grandfather for a long time. He was right about everything he said. But my thinking was going in a different direction. Maybe I was wrong as I reflected. I let my mind work. I thought that my grandfather was a male chauvinist, but I was wrong again. I think even in today's society the concept of the man will always conquer. Sometimes we do not admit that because we are selfish and feel superior. This is one of the principles that makes us men more strong than masculine. My adventure with the boss was not of extreme seriousness but was only the story of a young inexperienced fellow.

The hours went by and the darkness was falling It was a beautiful night to say outside, but it was late and my grandfather had finished his cigar. I could see that it was hard for him to keep his eyes open, but he didn't want to leave me. He wanted to hear the decision that I would make. After a few minutes of thinking I said: "Dear grandfather, I have been thinking about what you have told me. In this situation there are only two alternatives. The first is to leave my job. The second is to believe in the dignity of a man. I think I have a solution. To find a new job! I don't' have to worry about it. I have so much experience in my field that any company would be happy to have me. For my dignity, I think this is a gift. I truly believe that any man -- and for that matter any person -- that loses his dignity is lost, he is nobody in this world."

I stand up and lift my grandfather I put his arm on my neck and say, "Let's go inside. It's very late, have a good night's sleep. I hope tomorrow is a better day."

I give him a kiss and wish him a good night.

New Country

It was a day so hot that you couldn't breathe. The asphalt was so hot no one wanted to walk. The rays of the sun penetrated through the walls of the house. It was desolation everywhere. I thought, "The beach is not too far." At that moment my mind stopped completely and I said, "Run away, get out of here!" I started to think of my beautiful small town on top of the mountain where the air is so fresh and clean you could smell the air all day long. The freshness of the pine trees sent an intense perfume and sensation every time you took a breath.

It's not easy making dreams come true. Your mind plays with your body, the reality comes in front of your eyes. It is not a ghost, it's not imagination. Reality is a concrete observation of what is around me. My new country, the city in which I live, does not offer a lot of alternatives. I have one solution left, the beach. Not too far from where I live, there is an extensive amount of water, waiting with it are murmuring guests, small children, old people, young teenagers, people of different nationalities, a babble of voices speaking different languages. Sometimes you can even hear that sound penetrating into your ears. It sounds like a murmuring, you don't even care what it's trying to say. You just think your own thoughts.

the water. So I went to the top of a cliff at the extremity of the beach. It is not beautiful scenery, I mean not like my native country. I should never make a comparison, I have to accept what this country has to offer me, not illusion, just reality. The water at the beach is just water, it doesn't make any difference to me that it's calm or agitated. I can't do anything to change the daily expression of this enormous source of energy. The time goes through different waves of humanity. But the sea is always there, it doesn't move. If you look at the waves it's almost as if they are talking to you, like they're trying to tell you something. Finally this extensive source of energy calms, my mind starts to wander to a thought or an obscure idea. The daily problems vanish, I start to analyze in an instant. We humans are just a drop of water in this huge universe.

A new day takes rest on my tired shoulders. I lay at the guard rail that separates the sea's beach from the asphalt. The shore is full of simplistic people. They act as though they were in their bedroom getting undressed to get comfortable. They are not ashamed to show the world their nudity. You can see all different kinds of chests, legs, and different skin colors. It looks like a display of painted humanity that moves within a frame of a scene. All that human flesh packed together waiting its turn to be roasted by the merciless sun's rays.

I remember when I was a little boy and took walks in the small streets of my town I would pass by the butcher store and see all that meat hanging. It would hang from rusty nails, and the flesh and blood would attract flies all around to highlight the dinginess under the hot rays of the sun.

In an instant, I was feeling a sense of rejection by what I was observing. I had to turn my face the other way. I confess that the show I was seeing, all that flesh roasting from the rays of the hot sun, was giving me the creeps. I was trying to think of a way to exercise my vision. It was not right, even if we have a different idea. We can be realistic to accept that torture. Just think of the suffering that the human body endures. I am sure that anyone can arrive at the same conclusion that we all have the right to put ourselves in a position to alleviate all the suffering. Who am I to judge the human race? I do not have to accept what others want to do. If I don't like it I don't have to accept it. I don't have any other solution. I have to turn my vision to a different horizon. I look as far as I can and envision my country. I am sure that it hasn't lost the beauty that I left long ago. I decide to let my soul adventure into the new horizon, to new meadows and new frontiers. I talk to myself, I scream with my mouth open. I love my country, maybe someday I will see you again -- smell the perfume, see the beauty that I left so long ago. My body is the necessity that I need to survive here. I live in this new country that gives me happiness and sorrow. But my heart and mind are there on the other side of the ocean. That immense source of water that blocks my vision, I pray to God that my body survives the adversity that life has to offer, and that someday I will thrive, and that I can envision a time when I can relish the memory.

ALWAYS UNITED

"Always united" is a simple phrase to pronounce. It could be in anybody's vocabulary from the one you love to the politician. The meaning of these two words is of enormous importance. If we divide this phrase we will see that the word "always" refers to something infinite, and the word "united," meaning joined together, is of universal consequence.

Speakers put these two words together every day without thinking, without taking a breathe, and without reflecting on the outcome. Take, for example, a speech from an orator; he always uses this phrase to create an atmosphere of unification between himself and the people who hear him. The effect that he created when he pronounced these two words is worse than taking drugs or being brainwashed. When we hear these two words together, we feel full of prosperity, we feel high on ourselves.

How many meanings this phrase "Always United" has! I know a few people will greet this phrase with disdain and will say, "What's the meaning? There's no verb; there's no subject, it's just a pair of words out of context, not really clear. To complete the meaning you need other words." This is not a dilemma that requires fighting fire with fire. We don't have to squeeze our brain to find a better interpretation or solution. I reflect further and say "united" is a word which has a clear meaning: brotherhood, friendship, mutual respect, and a common intent to accomplish a solution.

Today the world is dying; it needs to be healed. We've got to love our world, we got to give a hand, a new breath of fresh air, new advice. The air that we breathe is polluted. It's not right that the world is full of detritus. Dust hides the garbage -- not just old garbage, but the new garbage that has been building up over the last century. We've got to make the dust disappear; a general clean-up is necessary. We must burn the past, burn the dirty residue of the past generation. Only by doing that we can clean up and heal this world for a better future.

"Always United." Not just today, but well into the future we've got to stay united more firmly than ever. We of the new generation that from nothing were created, we must defeat the ignorance, we must sacrifice our comfort. Our sons who got their maturity from us are now he ones that rule this society. We are still the ones that bear the responsibility on our backs. We still sweat carrying on to achieve our dream; but let's look at the reality in its substance.

"Always United" we must keep our faith high to carry on the dream and be united in this resurgence, and make sure that the people that rule this world have the same love for the human race -- summed up in the phrase "Always United."

Now, as tradition dictates, let's raise a glass to the sky and make a toast to prosperity and a better future. May this world which welcomes us for short stay, give us the bread and liberty. May we one day be a united realm full of brotherhood and peace and love for the whole human race. Only then can we honestly pronounce the phrase, "Always United."

Time Is Going By

In the small square of my town not long ago two best friends were talking about the life that they were living everyday. I saw them because they were sitting on one of the benches that had been there for an eternity. The color of the wood in the bench was faded from many years of sun and rain. I was sitting on the other bench enjoying my ice cream, I knew these two friends because we were all from the same town, and I saw them occasionally.

After a few minutes of talking I learned their names were Gianni and Paolo. They didn't notice anybody next to them, and they were talking very freely. From where I was sitting, I could not help but hear some of their conversation. So now I would like to tell you what I heard Gianni complain to Paolo:

"My dear Paolo I do not know what to do. Life is so meaningless and has nothing to offer anymore. I am thirty years old, I am still living at home with my parents. My mother with her old ideology complains that I am thirty years old and still not married, she repeats the same words every day. 'Gianni go out and find a wife, life gets short and you start to get old.'

Paolo, I know that my mother is right in every word that she says and I think that some day not far away I will listen to her. For now, I will talk with you because you are my best friend. Maybe I will ask one of my parents to help me out. You know me for a long time and you know that I am shy when something is very important. Maybe I will put an ad in the paper, but you know that already I talked with the priest of my congregation, and you know that today I am talking with you. I am still waiting for some answer. I am very discouraged; maybe something is wrong with me. Not long ago I was reading in the paper that statistics show that we men should not have any problem finding a woman, because there are more woman then men in the world. Statistics say that for every man there are seven women. To be honest, I do not believe in such statistics, and most of the time I don't believe what I read. But if this is true, we men should have no problem. For now I am still waiting, and I am surprised that no one has noticed me because I am still single. I do not understand why this has happened to me. I consider myself an unpretentious man, I do not ask for a lot, I am not too demanding. Do you know, my dear friend, that in my family they still believe and talk about dowries just like a hundred years ago. I do not believe in that, but if some woman were to come forward and want to get married, I would require that some interesting prospect came with her. I would like this woman to have some money already saved. I would like her to be a virgin and not have been used for past adventure. I would like her to be tall, beautiful, with a body that everyone would look at. I would like her to be very intelligent, with a sense of humor; and I would like her to be able to cook like my mother or better."

I listened to everything that Gianni said. Once in a while I was looking at his friend, Paolo, who so far just listened without interruption. I was waiting for Paolo to explode, but suddenly Paolo told his friend Gianni, "I hope you are finished. Now it is my turn -- and please give me the courtesy not to interrupt I am very serious about my reply."

Paolo took a few seconds to compose himself and then he started to talk. "My dear friend, Gianni, I hope you realize that you are in a deep dream, and I as your friend hope that you wake up as soon as possible. What do you have to offer this woman of your dreams who has everything that you ask? Why don't you look at yourself in the mirror and tell me what you see?"

Gianni was giving Paolo a dirty look; but he did not interrupt. Paolo continued, "I'll tell you, my friend, what you will see!" You will see a man with no future, a man tired with despair for a dream that never will be reality."

I heard that harsh comment and I was waiting for Gianni to jump at his friend. Instead Gianni responded with pride and a sense of humor. First he laughed, but it was a sarcastic laugh; then with a soft hoarse voice and with no conclusion on the subject in question, he said, "You are right, my dear friend! I am not the man that I believe to be, and I am tired of living this life. But for now I am a rare case because the men at the women's disposition are very few and I take advantage of the situation. I still have some value to offer; I am not an old man, my health is perfect; my sexual drive is enormous, and for that my value as a man is in demand. Also remember, my dear friend Paolo, today the women complain that they cannot find a husband that satisfies their complete demands. I think I have this capacity to fill their needs. I just have to wait, but I do not want to wait too long, I am starting to get tired of this life, I am tired of living with my parents and waiting in the corner for a dream that takes so long to become a reality. I hope that someone will come and wake me out of this dream. Time is going by very fast. I am starting to show some white hairs on my head. This really worries me,"

In the meantime, I finished eating my ice cream; but I did not want to leave. I was waiting to hear the end of the story. Just like that, I saw Gianni raise his head to the sky and say: "Please, women of this world, come! I cannot wait anymore. I do not care about statistics, I am alone, I am looking at myself in the mirror and I see wrinkles in my face. It is time to say I've got to stop, I've got to watch the reality, I can't go back in time. My mind is all confused from dreaming. I have only alternative to all this, and it is D-E-A-T-H!"

I saw Paolo get close to Gianni and give him his hand. Then I heard him say. "Let's go my friend," And they left..

My Friend the Ghost

When I first moved here, in the house I live in now, there was so much to do that I said to myself, 'Rudy are you sure you want to do all this work to make this place worth something some day'? I looked around the property again before I made the final decision and I said this is a challenge but I will buy this property.

There was a small barn behind the house that long ago was used as a bathroom, and, to be honest, I don't know why that, so-called, barn didn't fall to the ground. There were trees all over the place; the limbs littering the house, and the roof was covered completely; the house itself would have require major work. I knew all this work would take years of hard labor and a good amount of money.

The first month after I moved in I did a lot of walking, investigating, measuring, planning and thinking about what I would have to do to made things possible while I was planning the projects. I ask my longtime girlfriend if she would like to move in with me and help me, not physically but mentally about how to accomplish the difficult task to make the place look more attractive. I was very lucky that she said, 'yes', and I still am grateful to her for that; without her help I never would have accomplished what I had in mind.

Since the first day my energy began to rise; I felt that the possibilities were there, that helped me to start working every day on the project. My girlfriend was a busy nurse and her time to stay home and give me some ideas was very limited but when she was off work she would check around the house to see the progress of my projects and give me ideas – which was a plus because I believe that four eyes see better than two. The big projects were mine and I had to work fast enough to it done because the winter in these parts of the woods are very long and brutal. Ice storms, wind, snow, and sometime thunder storms bore down on the home. A few times when, at the end of the day, my back and arms ached, and I got back inside the house, I would ask myself why I was doing all that work; I retired to enjoy the rest of my life doing nothing but, in the end, I knew that I had to stay active to be happy; I knew that the pain the next morning would go away and I had to start work again. It turned out that we were happy about the progress on fixing the property the way we wanted it.

Our first year flew by fast and the place started to look very attractive; some of the neighbors stopped by to congratulate me about the work I was doing and that gave me more strength. The house was going to be a long project to finish; I knew that I would need more money because everything I wanted to do needed to be done by a professional; I had no special tools and in my life I never did anything to consider myself a carpenter – all my life the only job I had was in Aviation. I made planes fly safely; that was my job. So this was the reason I called a carpenter and talked to him about the remodeling of the house. The weather was too cold to start any work so we talked about what would be needed. I stopped work outside and all my free time I spent working at my new book of poetry that I love so much (and was able to finish in time to be published the next spring.)

The house had all the accommodations that we needed which was okay for the time being, we even put in a wood burning so as not to use a lot of heating oil because the price was very high.

It was one of those nights when the temperature was below zero that the fire on the wood burner needed more wood that usual; it was almost 10 o'clock and I knew that by 11:30pm my girlfriend would be home and I try to keep the house as warm as I could; I decided to go out and bring more wood inside. I turned the outside light on and as soon I opened the door I saw the shadow of a person go running in the back of the house! To be honest, I got scared and quickly returned inside the house and got my gun and a flashlight before I went out again and looked behind the house to see if anyone was there or if it was just my imagination. The moon was out which helped me have a better look. I went all around but I didn't see anyone so I got few logs of wood and went inside the house to make it warm for when my girlfriend would come home. It didn't take long after when she arrived home and started talking about her day at work; she asked me how my day went. I really didn't want to tell her about what 'happened' to me earlier but after a few minutes I had to tell her the story of 'the shadow' that I saw. After I finished telling her, I was surprised by the way she reacted to my story; it looked like she knew about it. I asked her why she hadn't said anything before this happened to me.

She just laughed and said that it isn't anything new; she had been seeing that shadow since we moved into the house. I jump up on sofa' and asked her why she had never told me about it. She didn't respond right away but after few minutes she said what would have been the difference if she had told me earlier?

She didn't finish her statement when, looking thru the window, I saw the same shadow that I saw earlier and this time it was knocking at the window!

I again got up and turned the outside light on and went to look outside but, once again, no one was there! On my way back inside the house I started to think to myself that, eventually, I had to find out about what we were seeing almost every night. Once inside I told her my intention was that the next day, in the morning, I would go over to the closest neighbor and ask about the history of the house that I just bought. That night we talked a lot about the event that was keeping us in suspense and the next morning didn't take long in coming. When the first light of the new day started to show in the house, I was very anxious to go see my neighbor but I first wanted to have coffee; I didn't want to disturb people so early in the morning. It was almost ten o'clock when I started to dress very warm because the temperature was almost below zero. My car was frozen and I decided to walk; it was just half of mile and to defrost the car

to Mass every Sunday and never giving any trouble to anyone. I have been living in this house for over fifty years and I knew them very well; they almost died at the same time." We were talking when John's wife sat next to her husband and introduce herself. "Hi Rudy, my name is Danna. Yes, like my husband told you, Frank and Mary were good neighbors: we really miss them! They died six years ago; first Frank died, he was very sick, and then Mary died less than a year later. They are both buried at the Cemetery not far from your house, that small Cemetery on the right when you drive to go down town. That is Carpenter Cemetery where all the family is buried. If you don't mind me asking you, why would you like to know the history of the property you bought"? I answered, "no reason, just curiosity; I want to thank you very much and, again, any time you guys want to stop by for coffee, my door is always open. I want to thank you for your time and for the information that you gave me. I better go back home before my girlfriend leaves for work. Thank you, again!" It doesn't take me long to get home and as soon I get inside I find my girlfriend was waiting for me, the first thing she said was, "Well, I can't wait to know what you found out about this house." "Wait a moment, I said to my girlfriend, while I pour myself some warm coffee", and I sat for a few moments before I told her everything that Danna and John told me. And I promised, Pamela, this is my girlfriend's name, that late that day I would have to take a ride to the Carpenter Cemetery to see with my own eyes if the tomb of Frank and Mary Carpenter was still visible. She agreed with me and after she left for work I drove to the Cemetery. I walked for a while.

I can tell that the place wasn't really kept the way it should have been but my reason being there wasn't to criticize the place but to find out more about Frank and Mary. It was cold but ten minutes after being there I spotted a headstone with the names of Frank and Mary Carpenter; it was hard to read but after I cleaned the headstone I was sure that it was what I was looking for.

I stayed there for five minute and talked to the tomb; I knew that both of them were listening to me because a few times when I closed my eyes, I was seeing the same shadow that was walking on my property and knocked at my window almost every night. I wasn't scared but a few times I had chills go thru my body. On that note I left the Cemetery, thinking about what to do the next time I would see the shadow knocking at my door or at my window. I waited for Pamela to came home from work and told her about what happened at the cemetery. It was eleven o'clock when she came home and she looked like she was excited to hear about my adventure at the cemetery. We talked for over an hour, sitting on the sofa in the living room, when all of a sudden we heard a knock at the door, the same knock that we had heard time and time again. I asked Pamela if she would like to come outside with me after I get a flash light and turn the light on, she said okay. We both put our heavy coats on and went outside. As usual, no one was there to see. But as soon we were outside I start to talk very loud. "Frank and Mary, I know that you are next to us; I know your story. I believe that you don't want us to live on this property that has been in your family for generations. Me and my girlfriend, we will never tell you to leave us alone, we are not scared that you knock at the door or at the window. I just hope that you like the way I fix it; I understand that it doesn't matter how many years go by, this will remain forever yours. Starting tonight, you are welcome to walk around and make sure that I will keep this property the way you would like. From now on, you two are my friends; your ghosts will keep me company for days and nights to come. Now, if you don't mind, Frank and Mary, we have to go inside because we are freezing!"

The end of the story tells you, never be afraid of a ghost that wants to be your friend – even if they have been dead for a very long time.

Poor People

It was a windy night in September. The sky was a little dark with a few stars shining next to the half moon. John and Dana came out from the small house they owned at the beach. They sat on the sand and watched the sea. The roar of the waves was not gentle, but John -- who was a fisherman -- convinced his wife that he wanted to go out to sea to fish at night . His wife tried to discourage him. She knew that the night was too dangerous to venture out to the sea by himself; but John reminded Dana that the next day the market was open for the sale of fish and that it would be a good opportunity to make some money for the family.

Dana knew that when John decided to go fishing no one could stop him, not even a hurricane. They were not rich, the only money the family lived on was the profit made from the sale of the fish. She understood that; and even if she loved her husband with all of her heart, she knew that this was his job.

John stood up from the sand, gave his hand to his wife, and started to walk back home so he could get ready to fish. The kids were asleep. John went near all three and kissed them, looked at them with fatherly love, and got all that he needed to go to the sea. He hugged his wife and said, "Do not worry, everything will be fine." Dana walked with him to the boat repeating the same words: "Please be careful. If something goes wrong, please turn around. We will manage. Please promise that you will do that." She knew that John was a very tough man and he could battle anything in the sea.

Before John put the boat into the water he recommended that his wife call Maria because she was sick in bed and maybe she needed some help with her two small kids. Dana promised her husband that as soon as she got home she would call. She wished him a good catch, gave him another kiss and made her way back home.

Inside the house it was very quiet. She went to look at her kids one more time before she called Maria. She warmed up some coffee that was left over on the stove and picked up the phone to call Maria. She dialed the number and let it ring, but nobody answered. Outside the rain started to fall. She thought, let me finish my coffee and I will call again. When she looked out the window next, the rain was coming down very hard. Every drop that hit the panes made a splattering noise. She thought of her husband every time a wave thundered onto the sand with horrific force. She finished her coffee and tried to call Maria again, but again nobody picked up the phone. She started to get worried. She remembered the promise that she made to her husband. She knew that Maria was living alone in that house and if anything should happen no one could help her. Her two kids were too small to understand that their mother was sick. They were poor like John and Dana, but they were good friends. When John could help her he was always there.

As time passed, she called a few more times but no answer. She decided to go see why nobody was answering the phone. She knew that it was raining like hell out there but she decided to go. She made sure that her kids were okay and left her house. As soon as she was out, a strong wind almost blew her to the ground. The lightning from the sky illuminated that dreadful night. She was scared, but she decided to keep going. She was praying every step that she took. She finally reached Maria's house. The broken door was half open. The water was going in from a broken glass window. It was cold inside. She looked inside and tried to find the switch to turn the lights on. A terrible scene appeared at her eyes. Maria was covered half way and one of her kids was on top of her bed looking at her. I got close and tried to wake her up. Maria, Maria!!! Maria!!! I was screaming but there was no response. I thought she was asleep. I decided to touch her forehead, she was as cold as marble. I took the child off the bed and the kid started to cry. The other kid who was asleep on the floor next to Maria's bed woke up and he started to cry. She got both of them in her arms and told them not to cry. Otherwise their mother might wake up. They didn't know that their mother was dead.

Dana was distressed but tried to compose herself. She said to herself, "I can't leave these kids here, I do not know who to call, Maria is dead and I can't do anything for her. I have to take these kids away from here." Dana's was thinking about the kids and nothing else. She reacted to everything that was going on in her mind. She made the Sign of the Cross over Maria, then covered her face, picked up the kids in her arms and left the house.

Outside the wind and rain were so strong that it looked like the end of the world, but Dana was a strong woman. She has been married to a fisherman for so many years that it made her a very independent woman. With Maria's kids in her arms she ventured into the storm to go back to her house. She finally reached her house

PDF59

where she checked that her own children were asleep. She changed Maria's kids clothes because they were all wet from the rain. Then she put them to sleep next to her kids. She was tired, and it was a terrifying night. She couldn't go to sleep. The idea that John was out there battling against the sea water made her nervous. The hours went by very slowly; but finally at the first light the door of her house opened very slowly. It was John. He thought Dana would be asleep and tried to get into the house without making too much noise but Dana was waiting for her husband to come back home. When John saw Dana he got close to her, kissed her and told her about his night.

"I battled against the sea all night, but now you see I am back with you and the kids. I am so sorry but I did not catch anything. It was terrible, I do not know what to say. I do not know what to do to get some food for you and the kids." Dana replied, "Please John, sit down and relax. We will manage. I know that you are trying your best to take care of the family. Your love is what we need right now."

After cleaning himself up John sat at the kitchen table. He sipped a cup of coffee and asked his Dana, "Did you go see Maria and how she was doing?" Dana looked at him; her eyes started to shine from the tears starting to come down. "Why are you crying?" asked John.

"Maria is dead," Dana replied! John scratched his head: "What happened to the small kids?"

Without answering her husband, Dana got up from the chair, took John's hand and said, "Come."

Dana and John went into the other room where the kids were asleep. As soon as John saw that there were five kids instead of three, he turned towards Dana and said, "You are a saint. God will protect you and all of our family because of you. We will keep Maria's kids because God will watch over us and even if we are poor, we will be a happy family."

THE FAKE SICK PATIENT

It is December; it is so cold outside that everything around is frozen. Frank is in bed with a fever so high that is sheets have to be changed every two to three hours because of the way he was sweating. However, tomorrow he will go to his family doctor and will ask him to try to cure is influenza with a shot of penicillin. He knows that many people do not believe in this system to cure themselves, but on the other hand many people believe that the modern cure does not work the way it should because the microbes are in the air that we breathe. There are so many microbes in the air that he can't tell the difference between them. Knowing this, each suffering patient has to come to his own conclusion.

Frank thinks that if you do not feel well you should go to the doctor, more importantly if it is influenza. When he goes to visit the doctor, maybe he will find other ailments. He knows that he getting old, but to be honest he do not complain for his health. He knows that going to the doctor is a mental obsession. Sometimes there is no cure out there to make anyone feel better. To be honest he can tell you that when he do goes to the doctor he feels better as soon he gets into his office, or should he call it a "studio". As he looks around the doctor waiting room, he can tell why his friend the doctor is not a cheap doctor, he can see in the studio armchair made of genuine skin, original painting hanging on the wall. He can see at each corner marble statues of very important personages. It looks like a museum. Every patient that goes to visit that doctor is shocked to see so much beauty.

Every time he goes there to be checked, he looks around, he sit and wait for his name to be called. In the time that he wait he thinks about this doctor, he is so genuine the way he receive his patients in such a comfortable environment! He can calm the patient's mind while he tries to deviate the illness from the body. Frank try to concentrate on the beauty of the room, but when he is too deeply ill he just sit and wait that day that Frank went to the doctor there were many patients before him and to make the time pass some of the patients were conversing. The studio looked more like a sociable bar than a doctor's office. It looked like everyone knew each other, that they had been friends for a long time. It was nice to see these people talking casually as he remember when he was young. Today it is not like that anymore; the new generation is so selfish, they do not care about sharing anything. He would like to give you an example: The other day he went to visit Joe one of his old friend he can see right away the coldness in the way Joe welcome him in his house no more brotherly talk, this is not because Joe likes to be like that, but because he is trying to adopt new ways of friendship. As always, Joe serves Frank in the kitchen where the outside door is very close, the wine, the nuts, the sausage and homemade bread are always there on the table, he didn't say anything significant, there is no communication, no courage to talk about what's going on in the world. No one wants to discuss the dirtiness of today's society. If you ask your best friend, and he can't give you a response, then the best thing to do is to drink some wine, eat some bread, and get lost for a few months before you see your friend again. If this is the way everybody acts, nobody needs a friend that cannot carry on a conversation. Where else do you go to have a conversation or to listen to the lately news? You could get sick (or if you are not sick just fake it) and make an appointment to go see your doctor. He is certainly smart enough to realize that the only reason you are there is to converse with the other patients or better, make new friends. The doctor knows the needs of the lonely person especially in this cold world that cares nothing about the needs of others. On that occasion of his last visit, even the doctor was very explicit (in a polite way, of course) and in his private office, he start to say: My dear friend, Frank you got to do me a favor, you can't come here and waste my time every time you need to converse with someone. You can see with your own eyes that I have many patients who are really sick and they are waiting to be examined I ask you to come see me just when you are sick. All the symptoms that you describe and the ones you complain, I can't do nothing about. You've got to live with them. It is normal for someone your age. But as a doctor and a friend I really have to be honest and tell you that the only problem you have is the way you express yourself with the other patients. They know that you tell them a lot of lies

The Marriage

Had been love at first sight, and in a short time they were convinced that they were made for eachother in a while they decided that it would have been opportune to get married. Rachel and John met over the summer in 1990. They were vacationing in Los Angeles, California. Rachel was from Bridgeport, Connecticut and John from Farfield, Connecticut. These two cities are very close to each other just a few miles apart. Since the first time that they lay eyes on each other they knew that something was there. They went out for a while, to the movies and occasionally to a bar to have a drink. And developed a sense of love so quick that after a few months that were back in Connecticut they decided to get together to discuss and figure out who was to meet the expenses for the wedding. The union as we know started with harmony, Rachel's family was very proud that her daughter found such a nice guy with his head on his shoulder and the same was for John's family, Rachel was very respectful toward all of them. She never went out with another guy before, John was her first man ever, everything was going well. But the day that everybody gather together to discuss the arrangement for the wedding the smile and the lips of both parents transformed. Everyone was saying their how story about coming up with the money to pay for the wedding. For a while there was a lot of yelling. Rachel's mother was very persistent about her family responsibility at what to pay for the wedding. John's mother was of the idea that because they were from Italy and like the old times the man in the family does not contribute for the wedding expenses. Anyway, it was just talk because after about an hour of talking they decided to split the expenses half and half. They saluted this decision with a good glass of wine that the father of the groom made at home.

John's father being very proud of his son and said:

This son of mine that I have brought up my way will have a good future, he is the one who will grow the family the old fashion way. I have taught him to respect love because it is something sacrosanct. Rachel's mother that of course adored her beautiful creature did not sit there with her mouth shout, this is more that right she replied, my daughter too, I have taught her the same lessons in life, I always told her to pay attention and watch out not to make mistakes in life because she would regret it some day, you all can see now this girl is the most beautiful and pure that you ever find. Rachel and John did not say a word during all of this discussion because they promised themselves to just listen and let the family talk then finally set the date for the marriage, for the following month. The day came, the wedding was beautiful lots of tears, the priest was very good, at the reception everyone could notice that the groom was becoming impatient, and very politely was trying to get rid with eachother, the time has come to tell you the secret because if I don't tell you now when we get in bed you will find out. It's something that can't be hidden, and I only pray God that you will forgive me. John that to the moment listened with out opening his mouth was astonished to hear his new wife talk like that, he don't know what to say his mind did not know how to react, until that moment he compose himself then he interrupted her, his eyes red from the rage, his blood boil out of his veins, but always composed say: this is clever, very clever and I that trust you with my life, you could have told me before the marriage that you are not a virgin, that you had an affair with another man before we met I would have understood. Wait a minute Rachel reply I am tired to hear all your accusations, just wait, if I told you when we met that I am a virgin it's because I am a virgin, and I am pleading not to force me to sin, John did not want to hear any reason, his rage was out of the ordinary, I don't believe you, you are trying to keep me calm, but I am a man of integrity, tell me what I'm going to tell my family about this. Please Rachel I don't want to hear anymore, tomorrow morning we go to church, we talk to the priest and the marriage will be dissolved, you will go back to your family, and my honor will be respected, do you understand that my dear Rachel? Rachel just looked at him, she was seeing John desperate, she started to smile full of joy, she got up and sit on his lap, kisses his head still sweating from the party and then with a soft voice say: John I don't know what you have understood, but let me be the one to tell you once again. That I always love you I am not one of those easy girls that give themselves easily, again she started to laugh. Dear John, what I want to confess you that at night in my sleep I snore very heavy, you never knew this because we never sleep together, I don't want that you would get upset over this, that's the reason I never told you, I don't want to disturb you in those nights that you are tired from working. John pulled a sigh of relief after Rachel explained, he hugs her, given her a kiss and then says: My dear wife please forgive me if I misunderstood I am so stupid (John with his strong arm made a move and lays Rachel on the bed, he gets on top of her and continues to say), for that it is no worry because you got to know that in my sleep I snore like a freight train... they both started to laugh they embrace very tight and in a flash they consumed their marriage to be husband and wife forever.

Divorced

It was Saturday, I woke up very early and made myself some coffee, picked up all my dirty laundry, and put it in the basket. After I finished drinking my coffee I picked up the laundry basket and went out to my car which was parked in the street. I put the basket in the back seat of the car and drove to the place that one of my friends had told me about.

It was a big room, really big! It was full of people, most of them men.. I looked all over and I thought I was in a factory full of machinery. I thought the noise would make my head explode. To be honest I didn't feel comfortable. Before my eyes I saw the continuous labor that these men were doing. They were working hard to get the laundry into the machines so they could get out of the noisy place as quickly as possible. The smell from this place was very distasteful. Between the perfume of the detergent and the stale sweat of the dirty clothes, the smell was making me light-headed. It was the first time I had ever watched this constant movement performed by these people, and it seemed pathetic to me. I watched for about half an hour and I didn't know what to think. I thought to myself that what

I was seeing would become a weekly ritual for me, too. In this time I put myself into reality. I sat down on one of the benches with my dirty laundry next to me and followed intensely what all these people were doing with simplicity. I thought to myself. "All these people are very experienced. Every single one of them is waiting for his turn to put the clothes into the machinery."

I watched to see if I could learn how to use these machines: for example, how much detergent should I put into the machine? How much change was required to start these machines? With no exaggeration, I thought it would be a very difficult task for an inexperienced man like myself. I felt obliged to learn how to do this stuff because I would end up doing this at the end of each week. I saw people reading the newspaper, people talking, having conversations about life, and keeping no secrets.. I thought to myself that no matter what was said there was no shame. I knew no one in this place because it was my first time here. However, even though I knew no one, I still didn't feel strange. They were all men like me who seemed to be doing their weekly washing. I was impressed with the way everything was functioning in order. The machines were nice and clean and were in a perfect line. To me it looked like a museum of contemporary art.

Since I was the last one to arrive, I had to wait to get a machine at my disposal. A gentlemen who noticed me waiting approached me and kindly offered me the machine he was finished using. I thanked him and realized what an adventure it was to finally have my first experience as a single man again. I put all my laundry inside the machine, then put the detergent and money into the machine. The machine then started to work. I then picked up a newspaper and sat down waiting for the machine to finish its cycle. A whistle would sound off to alert me when my laundry was done. Then I would pass the machine on to someone else.

I really wanted to converse with someone while I was waiting but didn't have the courage to start a conversation. I found myself observing again. Now time seemed to be going by slowly. I reflected about the past. My body began to tremble because I never thought in a million years that a man like me would be doing laundry on his own. I was always under the impression that this job was only for women. Obviously (and unfortunately), I was wrong because everyone in the laundry room was a man. That's when I realized that my concept was wrong. Finally, the whistle blew and my laundry was complete. At last I would be able to see if I could do the laundry right because I always thought this was an art only women understood.

I got up and began to take the laundry out of the machine. I was in shocked when I lifted the lid to see what a disaster I had made. All of my white clothes were different colors. At that particular moment I was very disappointed. I tried to hold my anger in and control myself. I was unsuccessful because a lot of vulgar words came out of my mouth. I wanted to break the machine. I didn't know what I had done wrong. My morale was very low. I was talking to myself, swearing and not understanding at what point things went wrong. People who had begun to fold their laundry were looking at me. They could see with their own eyes what I had done. All my clothes were different colors and looked like a rainbow shining inside this big room. A gentleman who was folding his own clothes was looking at me in a pathetic way, he saw what I did and that I was very disappointed. In a gentle manner the man approached me and excused himself. Then he held his hand out and introduced himself as Marc. He said he didn't notice what had happened. He then went on to say. "I don't want to give you sympathy or courage, but what happened to you has happened to all of us. It is very normal for this to happen. If it would make you feel any better, when I first did my laundry, I had to throw it out because I was in the same situation as you. I learned by myself how to do it right. Try to think in a philosophical way about what just happened."

An ironic smile just appeared on my face and I said, "I apologize, I didn't introduce myself to you. My name is Sal and it's a pleasure to meet you." Then Marc said that his laundry was done and he offered me help if I needed it before he left.

Before he left I asked him a question. Why are all these men here on a Saturday morning? In a gentle way Marc replied, "My dear fellow, all the guys you see here doing their laundry on Saturday mornings are divorced. It's safe to say that you are, too. We find ourselves here every Saturday not because we want to but because it's our destiny to be here. You will see, in time you will get used to this noise. You will get used to hearing all the complaining that everybody has to say about their ex-wives."

Marc stopped talking and looked at his watch. He said he was late and had to go. He had to go get his son. "God help me if I don't get there on time. My ex-wife will scream at me. I can't stand when she screams. Listen Sal, it was a pleasure meeting you. I'll see you next Saturday. I have to run.

I thanked him and he left. I was very happy to meet Marc. He elevated my morale with his words. However, I must confess that in that moment I was not thinking about the laundry that I had ruined. I was thinking about the future. The lessons I learned that day put me in a different position. I should start getting used to the things that are going to happen in my life. I had the impulse inside of me to speak my mind. Thinking of different lessons that the future held for me as a divorced man. Resignation was the first thing that came to my mind. I was perplexed and distressed yet I didn't want to accept the truth. I put my laundry inside the basket and went out to my car. I drove back to my humble apartment. I put the basket in the middle of the room and jumped on the bed to relax. I looked at the ceiling and thought about how many times I should go back to that place to wash away the sin I had committed against my wife. In her old-fashioned way, she would always make sure that I would go out clean into the world clean.

Then I fell asleep...

THE MIRACLE

In Rose a small town located north of the province of Cosenza, city in the region of Calabria, south of Italy, precisely in the district of (Turramuni) also refer to the (Ditch of the olive).

Francesco a citizen of this small town owns a farm, with plants of all kinds, but mostly olives trees. One day in April just about twenty years ago on the day of the (Pasquetta) a holiday that is celebrate in Italy the day after Ester. Francesco with his wife Maria and his children Gino and Roberto, and other friends decided to go in the beautiful orchard to celebrate that day in harmony, they had prepared everything from frittata (a mix of eggs, onion, sausage, and other spices) a Calabria specialty, to cotolette, home made bread, home wine, and other specialty, to continue all the goodness of God. They want to spend that special day without worries or thought of the days ahead, arriving at the location they look around to find a spot in the shade away from the rays of the sun, that in particular time of the year it is very hot.

Everything went accordingly to plan, they eat, they drank,

told old jokes, and even some stories that happened in town in the past, in other words the time went by in the best ways. At some time Francesco's wife got up and excused herself from the group saying that she need to take a short walk to digest all that food she had eaten, and also to exercise her legs a bit, for they had fallen asleep from sitting on the ground. Maria took a few turns in that paradise, admiring her well kept trees that every year give her and her and her family abundant fruits. The hours of that beautiful day went by fast, the sun start to hiding behind the mountain, although the sky was still alive with light, they all decided to take the way home, they gathered the remains, which I must say wasn't much for it had been consumed, Maria that come back from her digestive walk start to clean with the other women, the man wore intent to finish the last drops, of wine left in the bottles, Maria made sure that nothing was left where they eat, she really care about her property, it looks as if she was cleaning her dining room, they all joked about her insisting keeping everything in its place, and so after placing everything in the basket to bring home, they start to walk toward the town, they had not walked few hundred meter that Maria who was a little behind and admire again her property that look like paradise, notice a strange figure on top of one of her olive tree which was looking at her with eyes full of tears. She suddenly stopped, she looked again at the strange figure, she rubbed her eyes to be sure of herself thinking that maybe was the few glass of wine that she drank that made her see things, she called her son Gino that was walking few meter in front of her, she asked him to look closely at that particular plant of olive, and ask him if he can see anything different, Gino got close to the olive tree and he saw that image that his mother saw before him, he ran back and told his mother that what she saw was the image of Christ face in the olive tree. Maria and her son look each other, they want to call Francesco and give him the news but they knew that his health was not in the best shape, and by give him the news of this shape event that occur maybe he would have an hart attack and die right in there. But in the other hand mother and son can't keep secrets what they saw from the rest of the company, Maria told his son to keep looking at the image and that she would tell everybody, and that's what she did, she went to the group that was walking ahead of her and told them to stop and going back because she want to show them what she saw, the company went back and saw that same image, they wore some moment of disbelieving, they were admitting the face of Christ looking at all of them, Francesco wanted to assure himself of the truth and so he went close to the tree, the image was still there with the crying face, he fell on his knees right there in front that vision and start to pray, the friends also fell on there knees and start to pray.

The night was falling, and they had to return to town, they did not know how to start to recount what had happened, for sure there would be some people who would criticize, and say: they were telling tales to make them self more popular in the eye of the other citizen. The all group when they arrive in town stayed at Francesco house, they did not close one eye, but they prayed till the early morning light.

The bells of mother church begin to ring, it was time to go to mass, the people of the town who were used to the habitual daily rite usually were ready to go to church, but in this particular day, Francesco his family and friends all together as a big group went to church, the priest Don Giuseppe could not do less on seeing this big group entering together, and go direct straight to the chapel were the body of Christ was visable, they all nailed to the Cross, they fell on their knees and start to pray.

Don Giuseppe notice right away that some thing had happened during the night to have such big group of people came to church and act this way even if their faith was principally Christian. The mass began in its regular way, some time the faithful turned the head to observe the group on they knees praying without paying attention to holy mass that was being celebrate by Don Giuseppe even the priest time to time would give a look to notice some strange thing, doing by the group. The holy mass ended, the people start to leave but not before give the last look at the group in the chapel, they wore those who had to go work, those who got to go to the country to tend the animals or to work at the land, the women that had to go home and start the daily routine of house cleaning.

Some people remained for simple curiosity of seeing that group so intent in their praying Don Giuseppe after coming out the rectory where he had changed in his usual clothe of the day, went right to the chapel of Christ, recognize Francesco he call him to his side and have him explain there action even if it was something that pleased him very much to see much devote Christian, to see the goodness of the praying that was direct to the name of Christ. Francesco left the group praying and went with the priest in the rectory, so no one disturb them, Don Giuseppe, ask Francesco for an explanation, Francesco without hesitation start to tell Don Giuseppe what happened, even Don Giuseppe a priest of integrity in regard the faith of Christianity hearing the tale remained perplexed, but is faith was so strong that he ask Francesco and the other to take him to the location were Christ appear to them. Don Giuseppe and the group of faithful that had remained in church without hesitation start to walk toward the location of the miracle apparition. The curiosity was of extreme importance, they walk very fast step, and so in less than an hour they found themselves on the spot, Francesco point out to Don Giuseppe the spot were the tree was, and the image that he saw, Don Giuseppe ask the group to remain behind because he want to verify it by himself of the miracle.

He walked toward the olive he was sweating cold, things like that did not happen especially in the small town in the country, he inspect the tree, the figure of the face of Christ was easily visible, he made the sign of the cross, then he went back to see better than no other interference crated the image, he went close again he touch the face of Christ, his hand became wet from the tears that came out the face of Christ, at a point a strange sensation went through his body, he fell on his knees and start to pray, the group that he had fallow came closer to the tree and they fell in their knees and start to pray together with priest. In the mean time Gino, Francesco's son that had recognized that the miracle was real, without disturbing the praying started to walking very fast toward the town, arriving out of breath went directly to the police station, at his arrival he fond the Marshal, he told him the story, telling him that Don Giuseppe the priest was already there on the spot, the Marshal gathered few of his force, he made a phone call to the mayor of the town to advise some other authority and tell them what had happened and asked them to meet him in the district of (Turramuni). The Marshal and his man arrived on the location.

In a beat, they view the group of faithful praying without disturbing them they came closer together, they notice that Don Giuseppe was intense in his prayer. The Marshal told his man to stay back and inspect the zone, he on his own went closer to the tree, he inspected also he touched the face of Christ and he too got his hand wet with the tears of Christ. He did not want to believe in what he was seeing but a breeze of cold wild went through his spine, he look again at the image and kneel on his knees with the rest of the people and start to pray. The other police realize the truth and so they fallow the action of their commander and start to pray.

Meanwhile the mayor of the town, with the other authority, and some of the people that had some said in the every day life of the small town, like the doctor, the secretary of the mayor, the pharmacist, the teachers wore the people that formed the aristocracy of the small town, they all arrived on the spot and they could not believe their eyes when they saw the scene, Marshal, Police, Priest and so many other all there praying, the mayor and the others looked at each other and pray near the olive tree. The news of the miracle went fast, all curious wanted to see, to touch that image and realize the truth of that miracle that had graced that small town. Every one realizes that was not a vision, it was reality, and that Christ wanted to recompense those poor people full of faith paying them a visit. The echo of the prayers arrived in many far away lands, from the small town, the news scatter very fast, the Cardinal of the city of Cosenza, the journalists of many different newspaper, the television network, to make brief in less that on hour were all there, to see with their own eye what has happened. The faith of all these people with high respect united with these simple citizens all were praying nobody wanted to leave this Holy place. The night went by in prayer, next day all the daily newspaper dedicated the front page to the miracle that happened in Rose the small town that was not even on the map, but was in the heart of all the faithful that believe in Christ. Even today twenty or more years later the faithful of catholic persuasion and even some unbeliever bring themselves in the sacred place (given in memory of Francesco's family to the holy Church, to be sure that the faithful will go there and pray). As for me when this happened I was one year old, to tell them the truth, I don't remember but I am sure that my parents have spent many days in prayer in this Holy place. The time has passed I've had the good fortune to have came to the United State, I've returned to my small town many times and believe me that every time I went to that Holy place I pray, especially when I was in need of comfort and help. My faith towards the Catholic religion reinforces any time that I see or dream that Holy figure. I

My Friend Dann

Last week as usual I was sitting home by myself watching television that has been showing the same stupid news every night. I got mad, shut the television off and decided to go out of the house and go some place where I can see people or maybe see one or two of my friends. It has been very long time since I decided to go to a Bar and have few drinks. I knew from past experience that once I start to drink I can't stop and that can cause trouble not just in my life but also at home where me and my companion Pamela share a house together with my eleven year old son John. I reflected for a while before I got dressed and went downtown to one of the bars that for sure I would meet one or two of my friends. I really reflected about what I was going to do but then I said to myself I don't care what happens tonight I will go out to have few drinks.

The ride wasn't too long I knew the place very well and I took the short cut. The Eagles (that's the name of the bar) isn't a fancy place. The majority of my friends go there because there is no dress code, you can play pool, darts, and other games but the best thing is the music a good rock n' roll or country music that makes the place very attractive. When I arrived the place was half full, some of my friends where there, but also I saw a few new faces. Every body said hi and asked me where the hell I was all this time that I didn't go to the bar. John, the Bartender, an old friend of mine for at least 20 years never forgot what I drink and he filled my glass of my favorite Rum and Coke. (Capitan Morgan, my favor Rum and just few drops of Coke). Wow!! I was in heaven. I can go on all night long drinking Capitan Morgan and Coke and bullshit with my friends talking about life, politics and of course family. No work for a change. People were coming and going during the evening. Time was flying. I knew that in a few hours I did my share of drinking and I started to feel very happy about it, I don't want to leave.

It was little after midnight and the place start to empty. My friends had left to go home where for sure there families where waiting for them. I had no intention to go home and all too soon my good friend Dann opened the door of the bar. As soon I saw him I give a good welcome with a high voice, "Dann what hell are you doing here at this time of the night? Did you lose your way home? Or did Jenny (his wife) throw you out of the house? John please give my friend Dann a drink to keep me company and maybe he will tell me what hell he's doing here at this time of the night."

Dann after few sips started to talk by telling me that he called my house to ask a question and that Pamela my companion answered the phone. I interrupt Dann) Pamela answer the phone? But she supposed to be at work that was the reason that I went out in the first place. The fumes of the alcohol start to make my brains very active and I start to ask lot's of questions. "Come my friend tell me what Pamela said? Did she tell you that I was here at the Eagles having a few drinks and for you to come over and take me home just in case I can't drive? Come on tell me the truth. For now I don't want to go home, and you as my best friend should not take me home, and when I decide to go home I will come up with an excuse, I can't take it any more with my family obligations. I can't let Pamela stay awake waiting for me every time I go out because she knows that I like to drink and get drunk. No tonight I will not go home and you my friend, don't leave me. Let's have few more drinks don't worry I'll pay. Hey John do you have some thing to eat? The drinks go down better when I have something in the stomach. It has been some time since I started to get tired of my way of living, and I want to thank you guys to hear my complaints. When I am home and talk with my son I am ashamed because some day he will find out that I am an alcoholic and just think about that makes my life worthless. That is the reason that at times I don't want to see anyone and disappear and go far way.

My friend do you hear the bells of the Church, the sun is rising please don't take me home now. I ask for more company, some time a friend is more than a member of the family. Do you guys know that my son is in the 6th grade, and when he has homework he starts to ask me to help him, and I start to feel like an idiot. How am I going to tell him that I never went to school, and I never hold a job, I try a hundred times but after the three months of training I always get fired. Maybe I am not that kind of person made to go to work, but I am still a lucky man because I live with my girlfriend's money and she loves to go to work. Sometimes it is better that I forget about having a family because as a man I'm worth a penny. I got to keep my mouth shut and the only thing I can tell my son is to go to the bathroom before going to bed. I swear if things continue this way I will going crazy, can't drink and do nothing every day of my life.

Dann, you are the right man to have a family. You are a good father and good husband, and please forgive me that I beg you to stay with me and don't take me home. I love you all, I swear, all of you are in my heart, I don't want to make things worse. Pamela is always awake and when I get home always ask what hell I did, she never mistreats me. Actually she sits at the kitchen table and laughing, she asks how many drinks I had, and like a good woman she fries me two eggs and a toasted bread to make sure I am okay. Poor woman, I disappoint her this is one reason to not go home. I see my friends you have been watching the time, yes is late and it is my fault. You know the duty of having a family and after this long night spent with me you will go to work tired as hell. But believe me what happened tonight was very beneficial to my life finally I had a very good friend to hear me. I feel much better and with my mind less confused. I believe that now is the time to go back home. Pamela will be offended only for a minute, as soon she sees me she will be more relaxed and she will go to work with peace of mind. And after the kid leaves for school I got to go to the market. I always did that since I met Pamela, and when she is in the kitchen cooking she always says that nobody can shop like me and spend less money. And if we eat so good it is because me, and that makes me happy, isn't anything big I know that, but his something that Pamela appreciates that makes her forget everything that I do contrary to the family activity.

Now my friend this is the last story, please give me a ride home today is a new day. John thanks for keeping the bar open all night.

Printed in the United States
by Baker & Taylor Publisher Services